Mij Kelly Mary McQuillan
Nursery Time

Hodder
Children's
Books

A division of Hachette Children's Books

This is the story of Suzy Sue,
who went away...

...who knows where to!

Her friends searched
the **hen house**.

They ransacked
the **sty**.

They called her name.

There was no reply!

They searched all over, high and low.

But the dog with his nose knew just where to go...

The cow read the writing. "Oh, me! Oh, my! The child's gone to nursery," she said with a sigh.

She crossed her front legs
and pulled a glum face.

"What's wrong?"
cried the hens.

"What's **wrong** with this place?"

Sunshine
Nursery

"Nothing's wrong," said the cow. "In fact, it's just right.

It's a perfect playground of children's delight!

It's full of **toys** and **paint** and **glue**.
It's just the place for Suzy Sue.

No doubt she'll make all sorts of friends!"

"That's **really** good!" said one of the hens.

"Don't be so sure," grumbled the cow.

"Do you think Suzy Sue will **come home** to us now?

She'll like it so much, she'll **never** come home. We'll be stuck on the farm all **on our own!**"

Oh, what a disaster! Oh, what a blow!
The dog cried, "Alas!"
The horse gasped,
"Oh no!"

The goat wiped his glasses, his voice was unsteady.

"I miss her," he bleated.
"I miss her already!"

"We **must** get her back," decided the sheep.
"Yes," said the cow. "We can't stand here and weep,

sniffling and snuffling, getting sadder and sadder."

The sheep was already knitting a ladder.

They came through the window.

They came in disguise.

The hens went ahead, acting as spies.

"We're going to check the children's shoes

till we find the ones that are Suzy Sue's.

We'll take her home, where she belongs."

But then their cunning plan went wrong.

"Oh my word! Is that **real** pretend money?

"Take a look at this book. It's ever so funny

"Look what I made. A cardboard box boat."

"Do you think it will sink?
I think it will float."

"We've changed the plan," announced the cow.

"We're going to stay forever now.

We love this place, and so will you.
There's so much here to see and do."

"There are loads of **pictures** on the walls.

There are shelves of books and **bouncy balls.**

There's water, sand and building bricks,

and songs to sing and cakes to mix,

and — oh my goodness —

Suzy Sue!

Well, fancy running into you!"

But Suzy Sue said,
"Dearie-dear.
You're **far** too **big**.
You **can't** stay here.

This place is specially designed with children just like me in mind."

Oh what a **blow!**

The dog started to weep.

The hens threw themselves

in a heart-broken heap.

"But if we have to **go** and you're going to **stay**, we'll **never** see you!" they cried in dismay.

"Of course you'll see me," said Suzy Sue.
"This isn't my home. My home is with you.
I'm not going to live here, I just come every day.
I play for a while and then go away."

Well that was such a **big** relief,
they all went home, forgot their grief.

They thought about what they'd learned.
They made a **plan,** and then they turned
the farm into a place designed
With **all** the things they liked in mind!

That was the story of Suzy Sue
who goes to a nursery –
and lives in one too!